IF YOU WERE A KID AT ELLIS ISLAND

BY JOANA COSTA KNUFINKE • ILLUSTRATED BY LEO TRINIDAD

CHILDREN'S PRESS®

An Imprint of Scholastic Inc.

Special thanks to our consultant, Matt Housch, Archivist at the Statue of Liberty National Monument, for making sure the fiction text of this book is authentic and the nonfiction text is historically accurate.

NOTE TO THE READER, PARENT, LIBRARIAN, AND TEACHER: This book combines a historical fiction narrative with nonfiction fact boxes. While all the nonfiction fact boxes are historically accurate and true, the fiction comes solely from the imaginations of the author and illustrator. The author and the editors acknowledge that, during this same time period, the experiences of kids from races, ethnicities, and/or backgrounds other than the ones featured were extremely different.

Library of Congress Cataloging-in-Publication Data available

ISBN 978-1-5461-3625-5 (library binding) / ISBN 978-1-5461-3626-2 (paperback)

10 9 8 7 6 5 4 3 2 25 26 27 28 29

Printed in China 62
First edition, 2025

Book design by Kathleen Petelinsek

Photos ©: 9: Shutterstock; 11: The Print Collector/Alamy Images; 13: Richard Cummins/Alamy Images; 15 exam: The Granger Collection; 15 hook: Jennifer Booher/Alamy Images; 17: National Park Service; 19: The New York Public Library; 21: Spencer Platt/Getty Images; 23: Louise collection/Alamy Images; 25: The Statue of Liberty-Ellis Island Foundation, Inc./National Park Service; 27: Robbin Merritt/Flickr.

TABLE OF CONTENTS

A Different Way of Life

Most people in the United States can trace their origins to somewhere else. This means that either they or their ancestors were **immigrants**. During the early 20th century, most of these newcomers entered the United States through Ellis Island. It is estimated that this **immigration station**, situated on a tiny island in New York Harbor, welcomed at least 12 million people to America during its years of operation. Most of them arrived after many days of traveling on **steamships** coming from harbors around the world, mainly from Europe. They spoke many different languages. Some were running away from poverty, war, or **persecution**. Others were simply looking for new opportunities. The story of each of these people is unique. But there is something most of them shared. They were hoping for a better life in America.

Turn the page to visit this important place in American history, and share in the struggles, fears, and hopes of millions of Americans.

Meet Isabella!

This is Isabella! She is originally from a little town outside Naples, Italy. Her papà left home to go to America three years ago, when the fields her family owned stopped giving them enough food to eat. While her father was away, her mother sadly died. It is now the summer of 1907, and Isabella is sailing on a steamship to New York to finally join her papà in America. She is not alone. She is traveling with her little brother.

Meet Alberto!

This is Alberto, Isabella's little brother. He is sad to have left his town, the only place he has ever known in his entire life. He really misses his mother, and he is afraid that, in America, he will also miss his family and friends who stayed in Italy. To top it off, he has been sick for the last three days on the ship. He has a headache and chills, and he is feeling very tired. He just wants to go home, but . . . where is home now?

Isabella stared at the horizon. A little shape came into view. "Look, the Statue of Liberty!" she exclaimed. The **monument** slowly became bigger. All the third-class passengers around her began to shout with excitement. All except Alberto.

"I don't care," he said. Isabella could feel Alberto was upset. And he was clearly not feeling well. Isabella thought about their papà. She could barely remember his face. But she remembered how his hugs felt. She could not wait to see him!

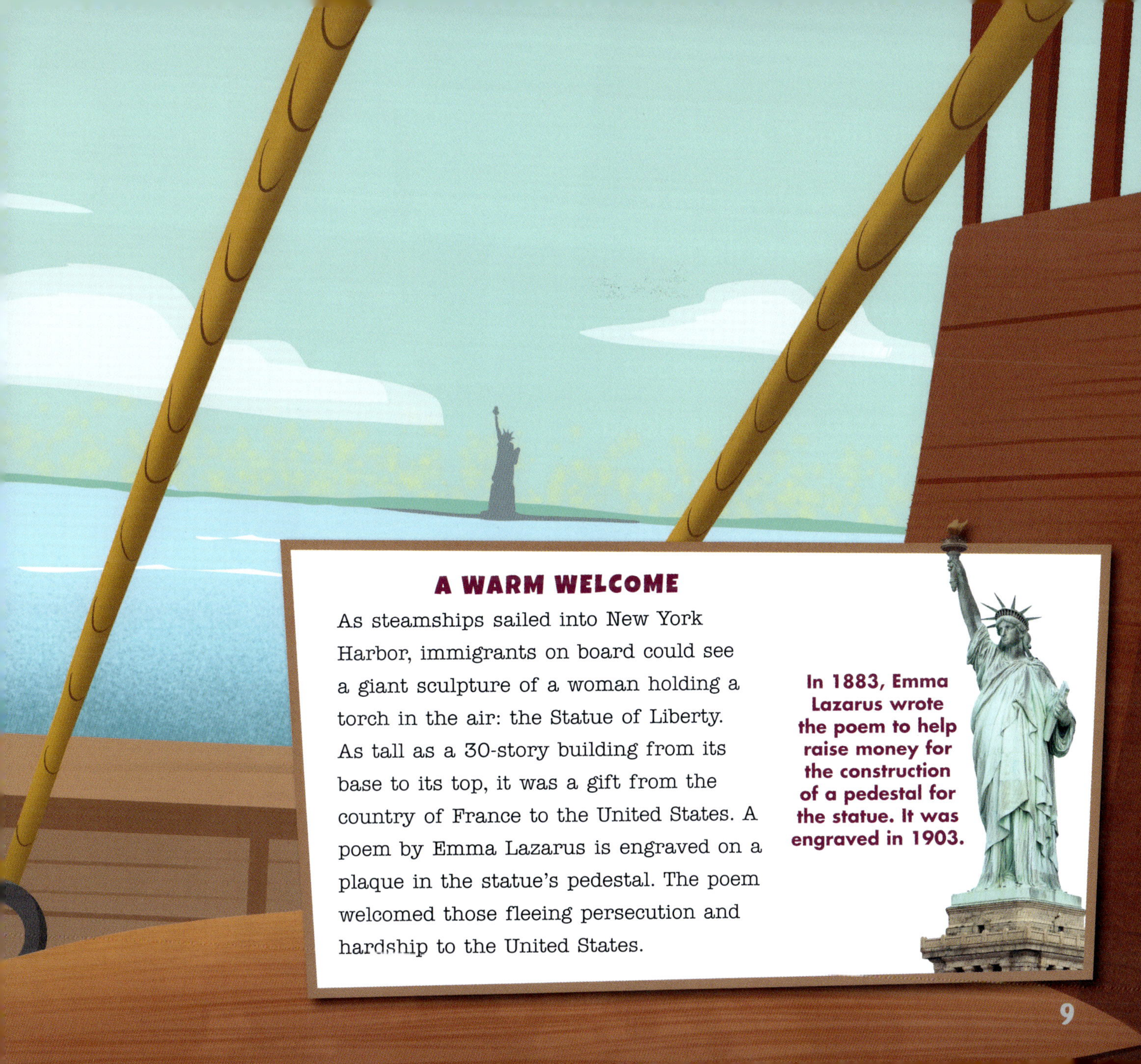

A WARM WELCOME

As steamships sailed into New York Harbor, immigrants on board could see a giant sculpture of a woman holding a torch in the air: the Statue of Liberty. As tall as a 30-story building from its base to its top, it was a gift from the country of France to the United States. A poem by Emma Lazarus is engraved on a plaque in the statue's pedestal. The poem welcomed those fleeing persecution and hardship to the United States.

In 1883, Emma Lazarus wrote the poem to help raise money for the construction of a pedestal for the statue. It was engraved in 1903.

"Is this Ellis Island?" asked Alberto as they were struggling to get off the boat and onto the pier.

"No, not yet!" said Isabella. Before the trip, they had rehearsed many times what to do at Ellis Island. No matter what, they had to act as if everything was fine. They had to pretend they were calm and happy. They both knew Ellis Island was the place where some people were sent back home, and they wanted to avoid this. Both kids followed the crowd until they joined the line for the ferry.

ISLAND OF HOPE, ISLAND OF TEARS

First- and second-class passengers were dropped directly at the dock in New York Harbor, and most of them were free to go. But passengers traveling in third-class, or **steerage**, who had paid less for their tickets, were taken by ferry to Ellis Island. It was here where agents would decide if the immigrants were allowed into the country . . . or if they would be **deported** and sent back home. The agents deported people who they thought would be unable to work, or who carried diseases that could spread in the United States.

About 2 out of every 100 immigrants were deported.

"Isabella, I really don't feel well . . ." said Alberto with a tiny voice.

"Don't worry, I can carry your things for you. But please just pretend you are calm and happy, like we practiced." But it was too hard. Alberto now felt so sick that he had to sit down on the suitcase he was trying to carry.

"Stand up, Alberto. Let's leave our stuff in the baggage room!"

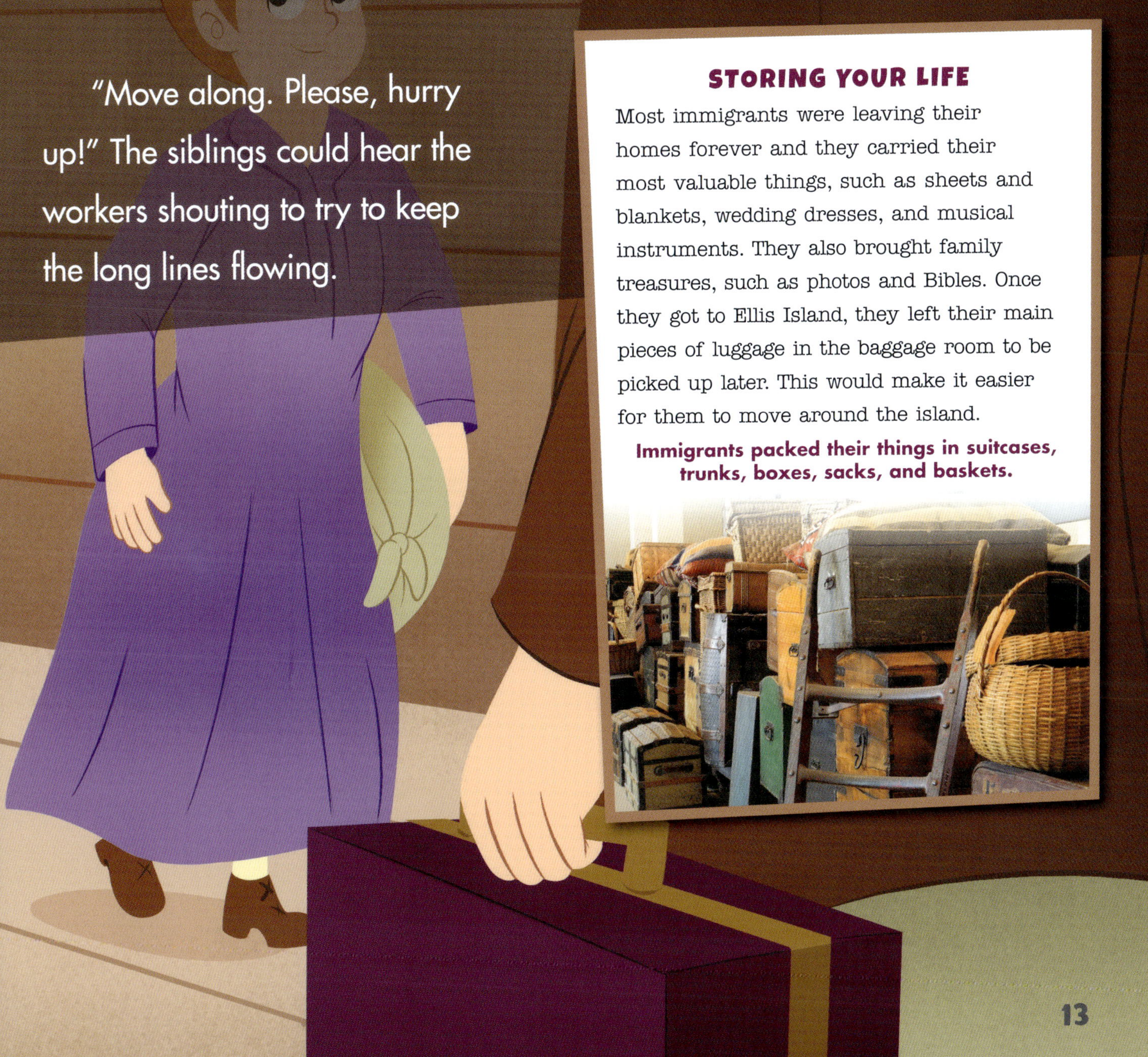

"Move along. Please, hurry up!" The siblings could hear the workers shouting to try to keep the long lines flowing.

STORING YOUR LIFE

Most immigrants were leaving their homes forever and they carried their most valuable things, such as sheets and blankets, wedding dresses, and musical instruments. They also brought family treasures, such as photos and Bibles. Once they got to Ellis Island, they left their main pieces of luggage in the baggage room to be picked up later. This would make it easier for them to move around the island.

Immigrants packed their things in suitcases, trunks, boxes, sacks, and baskets.

"**Inspection** is that way," shouted a staff member, pointing toward the stairs as the two siblings were leaving the baggage room. *I need to pretend I am calm and happy*, thought Isabella. She was holding her brother's hand tightly to help him climb the staircase when a doctor came closer. Suddenly, he marked Alberto's back with a piece of chalk. "This child needs a full medical exam!" the doctor exclaimed.

Isabella felt a rush of fear. Alberto was taken aside, and she was asked to continue walking.

THE HEALTH INSPECTION

On the second floor of Ellis Island's main building was the registry room, also called the great hall. There, immigrants had to go through a very quick medical exam. Doctors checked their hands, faces, eyes, necks, and hair in search of signs of diseases such as tuberculosis, cholera, and others. If people did not pass the exam, they were marked with chalk on their backs and pulled into special rooms for closer inspection. Some people were marked with chalk and pulled aside even earlier, as they were going up the stairs.

During the health inspection, the buttonhook (right) was used to check for bumps under the immigrants' eyelids. This was a sign of trachoma, a disease that spread easily.

Isabella had been separated from Alberto for what felt like many hours when an officer finally called her. He had a big notebook, and he asked her many questions: "What is your full name? What country are you from?" Thankfully, there was an **interpreter** helping Isabella speak with the officer. She answered every question and explained that she needed to contact her father to let him know she and her brother were finally here, at Ellis Island. "I also need to know what happened to my brother," she added.

ASKING QUESTIONS

The next step was the legal examination. Immigration officers had the ship's **manifest** in front of them. It had been completed in the country of origin before the ship left the harbor. With the help of an interpreter when needed, the officers asked the usually nervous immigrants different questions. Then they checked their answers against the information that appeared on the ship's manifest. An incorrect answer could be a reason for deportation.

The manifest listed all the people who had been on the ship, their age, their country of origin, and many more details about them.

"Your brother is sick, and he has been taken to the hospital," said the interpreter. "You must now remain at Ellis Island. Please, move down the stairs and somebody will help you."

Isabella felt very confused. There were so many people! The room was so noisy! She was hungry and thirsty. She overheard somebody talking about food being served in the dining hall by the entrance. Isabella used her last bit of energy to go there.

UNFAMILIAR FOOD

Most people stayed at Ellis Island for only a few hours. But others were **detained**. This meant they had to stay there for days, weeks, or even months. To feed them, food was provided at the dining hall three times a day. Usually, nourishing foods and drinks, such as baked beans, boiled beef, hard-boiled eggs, and milk, were provided. However, for many immigrants the food was unfamiliar. Some people tried ice cream, bananas, or spaghetti with tomato sauce in this dining hall for the first time.

The food at the dining hall was paid for by the steamship companies.

As she sat eating, Isabella wondered if Alberto had gotten dinner. Tears filled her eyes.

"Don't cry anymore." A tall woman sat by Isabella's side. "My name is Antonia, and I am here to help you," the woman said. She worked for an organization that helped Italian people going through Ellis Island.

After dinner, Antonia took Isabella to a very large room. "You can now make your bed and rest," said Antonia, handing Isabella a set of sheets.

In just a few minutes, Isabella fell asleep.

A PLACE TO SLEEP

People who had to stay at Ellis Island also needed a place to sleep. They were given spots in dorms around the island. Dorms usually consisted of long rows of three-level bunk beds that could be folded during the day and set up at night. When bedtime came, immigrants received blankets to spread over the thin canvas mattresses. Dorms were divided by gender, and there were smaller units to be used together by detained families.

The many dorms were filled almost every night.

Antonia woke Isabella the next morning. "Today we'll write a letter to your papà to let him know you are here. And you will be able to visit your brother at the hospital."

"Alberto! I missed you so much," Isabella said when she finally saw him. Over the next few days, her brother felt a little better every day. Now, he even wanted to learn things about America. Isabella read him books from Antonia's library.

Isabella also found other kids to talk to. But the days felt very long. There wasn't a lot to do on the island but wait.

PEOPLE AT WORK

Many people worked at Ellis Island to make sure things ran smoothly. Hundreds of doctors, nurses, clerks, interpreters, janitors, and kitchen and laundry workers were on staff. There were also organizations that had offices on the island and helped people from specific countries or religious groups. They gave immigrants warm clothes and food. For children, they provided music, games, and treats. They also helped kids traveling alone connect with family members who were already in the country.

A group of immigrants writes letters around a table at Ellis Island.

One morning, two weeks after their arrival, Isabella ran to Alberto's bed at the hospital. She was so excited she was out of breath. "You will be out of here very soon! And Papà will come and pick us up!" she exclaimed. Earlier that morning, the doctors had said that Alberto just needed two more days to fully recover from **typhus**. And a letter from their father had announced that he would pick up the kids at Ellis Island that same day.

IN GOOD HANDS

The hospital at Ellis Island grew to have 15 buildings and about 500 beds by 1907. Doctors and nurses treated all sorts of diseases there. They took care of immigrants who were sick upon arrival before letting them enter the United States. After being cured, they were allowed into the country. However, immigrants with certain diseases such as trachoma were directly sent back to their home countries without going to the hospital.

Doctors and nurses also helped pregnant women have their babies. About 355 kids were born at the hospital at Ellis Island.

Isabella noticed she had goose bumps when she saw her father walking down the path. *He looks exactly the same,* she thought. She ran toward him and threw her arms around his neck. Alberto shyly followed her and joined in.

As their father hugged them back, he said, "I am so happy you are here with me, in America!" Isabella closed her eyes and savored her father's warm hug.

"Where are we going, Papà?" asked Alberto.

As they all left Ellis Island, calm and happy, their father finally answered. "Home, Alberto. We are going home."

A NEW LIFE BEGINS

When immigrants were told they were free to go, they had a few things to do before leaving Ellis Island: exchange foreign money for American money, purchase railroad tickets if they needed them, and retrieve their baggage from the baggage room. Some immigrants stayed in New York. Others went somewhere else beyond the city. No matter how long they had been at Ellis Island, they probably felt very relieved after being let go. The door to America had finally opened!

These are called the stairs of separation. Each staircase took immigrants to a different destination: detention, the dock in New York City, or places beyond the city.

MAP

Ellis Island

For centuries, the Lenape People harvested oysters for food from the shallow waters around Ellis Island. They called the island Kioshk, which means "gull island." During the late 19th century, the U.S. government turned the tiny island into an immigration station. The number of immigrants coming through Ellis Island quickly grew, and the island was made larger to create more space. Its current size is 27.5 acres, about the same as 15 soccer fields.

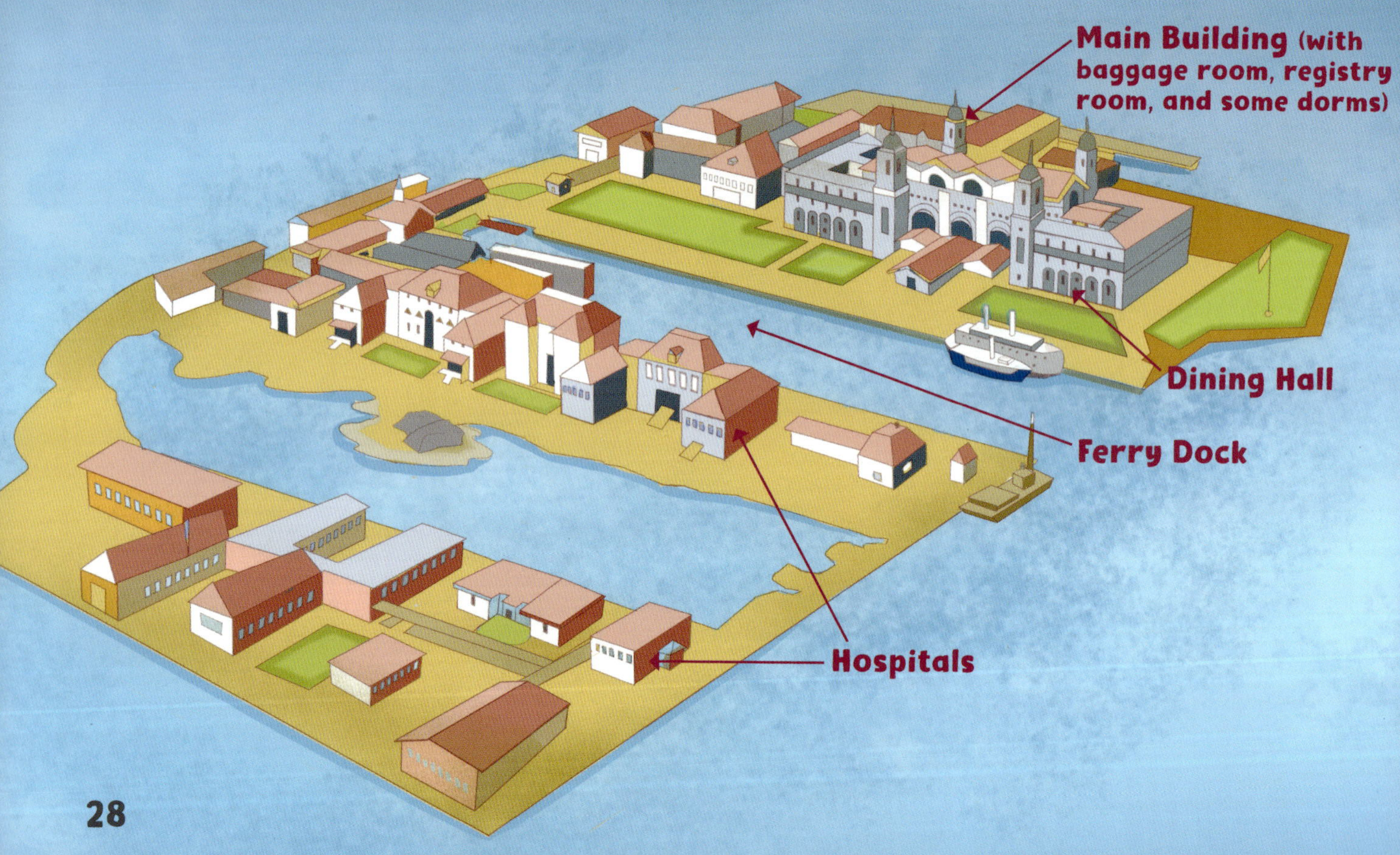

TIMELINE

1892 The immigration station at Ellis Island opens.

1907 Ellis Island processes more than one million immigrants that year, setting the record.

1910 Angel Island Immigration Station opens in San Francisco Bay. It will mainly process immigrants from Asia. It will operate for 30 years.

1921 New laws limit the amount of people that can come to the United States every year to 350,000.

1943 All the manifests of ships that arrived at Ellis Island are microfilmed. Five years later, the manifests are destroyed.

1954 The immigration station at Ellis Island closes its doors.

1965 President Lyndon Johnson names Ellis Island a national monument.

1973 Interviews with immigrants who entered the country through Ellis Island start to be conducted and are added to an oral archive.

1990 Ellis Island opens as a museum. It welcomes about three million people every year.

2001 The digitized manifests are made available to everyone online.

Today Millions of people from around the world continue to leave their countries of origin every year and come to the United States in search of new opportunities.

WORDS TO KNOW

deported (di-POR-tuhd) sent back to their own country

detained (di-TAYND) held back when they want to go

immigrants (IM-i-gruhnts) people who move from one country to another and settle there

immigration station (im-i-GRAY-shuhn STAY-shuhn) a place designed to process immigrants arriving in a country

inspection (in-SPEK-shuhn) a careful look at something or someone; an examination

interpreter (in-TUR-pri-tur) a person who translates a conversation between people who speak different languages

manifest (MAN-i-fest) a document listing the cargo, passengers, and crew of a ship or vehicle, for the use of customs officers and other officials

monument (MAHN-yuh-muhnt) a statue, building, or other structure that reminds people of an event or a person

persecution (pur-suh-KYOO-shuhn) the act of continually treating a person cruelly and unfairly, especially because of their ideas or political beliefs

steamships (STEEM-ships) ships powered by a steam engine

steerage (STEER-ij) the part of a ship that provides accommodation to the passengers with the cheapest tickets

typhus (TYE-fuhs) an infectious disease carried by lice, fleas, mites, and ticks that can cause headache, fever, and rash in humans

INDEX

ABOUT THE AUTHOR

Joana Costa Knufinke is originally from Barcelona, a beautiful Mediterranean city. She moved to the United States, sponsored by a Fulbright scholarship, in 2010. She remembers it was hard to leave family and friends behind, but at the same time, she was excited to start a new life in New York City. Today, she lives with her husband and two daughters in Brooklyn and works as an editor for Scholastic. Her Catalan language and culture have moved with her to her new home.

ABOUT THE ILLUSTRATOR

Leo Trinidad is a *New York Times* bestselling illustrator and animator from Costa Rica. For more than 12 years, he's been creating content for children's books and TV shows. His short form series have aired in more than 40 territories around the world on channels such as Disney and Cartoon Network.